DINOSAURS

Written by Anne McCord
Series Editor Lisa Watts
Editorial revision by Margaret Stephens
Consultant Editor Dr L. B. Halstead
Designed by Graham Round
Design revision by Linda Penny
Illustrated by Bob Hersey and Robert Morton

Contents

What is prehistory?

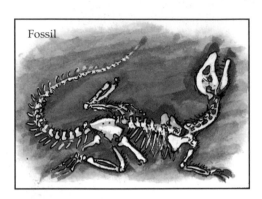
Fossil

Iguanodon

The remains of animals and plants which lived millions of years ago are called fossils. Scientists study them to find out the story of the Earth before people lived or could write down history. This story is called prehistory.

During prehistory, about 150 million years ago, strange creatures called dinosaurs lived on Earth. We know about dinosaurs and how they lived because their fossil bones have been discovered, buried in the rocks.

Dinosaurs form only one chapter in the long story of prehistory, because the Earth is about 4,600 million years old. You can make the time dial below, to help you follow this story. It will show you how life on Earth began.

Make a time dial

You need some cardboard, tracing paper, a paper fastener, felt tip pens and scissors.

This big circle is the pattern for your time dial. Trace it onto the cardboard. Make sure you mark the middle and all the rectangles.

Now trace the circle again. This time trace only the middle and the two red rectangles.

Colour this circle.

Draw a tab.

Cut out the circles, leaving a small tab on the one with all the rectangles. On the other circle, cut out the two red rectangles to make little windows.

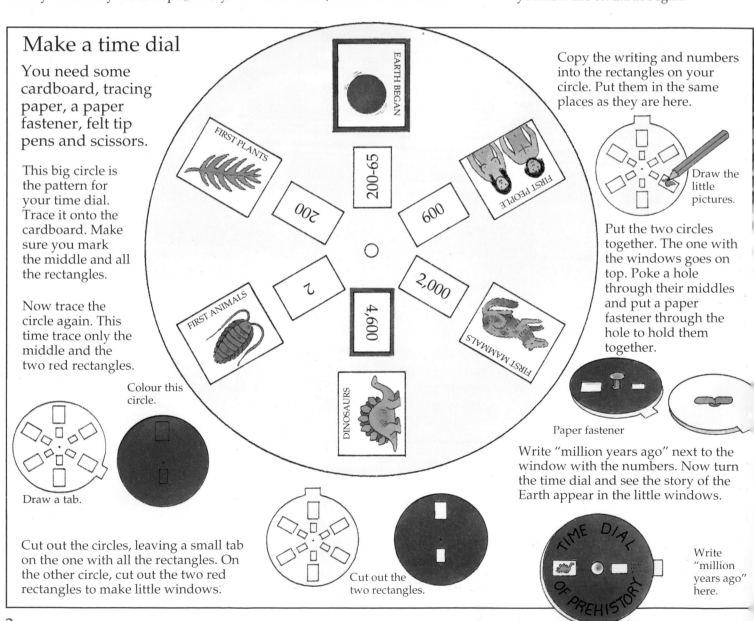

EARTH BEGAN

FIRST PLANTS

200-65

200

600

FIRST PEOPLE

2

2,000

FIRST ANIMALS

4,600

FIRST MAMMALS

DINOSAURS

Cut out the two rectangles.

Copy the writing and numbers into the rectangles on your circle. Put them in the same places as they are here.

Draw the little pictures.

Put the two circles together. The one with the windows goes on top. Poke a hole through their middles and put a paper fastener through the hole to hold them together.

Paper fastener

Write "million years ago" next to the window with the numbers. Now turn the time dial and see the story of the Earth appear in the little windows.

TIME DIAL OF PREHISTORY

Write "million years ago" here.

How the Earth began

Scientists have studied the Sun, the other stars, and the rocks of the Earth to find out how our planet formed. They think that about 4,700 million years ago Earth did not exist. There was only a huge cloud of dust and gases swirling around the Sun. Then the cloud split up to form several small clouds. Each of these probably became one of the planets which now go around the Sun.

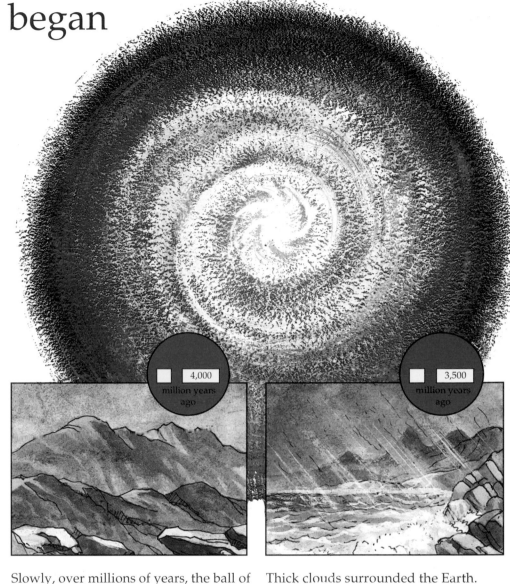

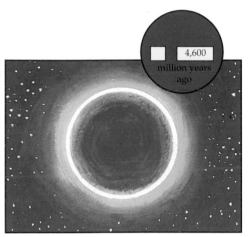

4,600
million years
ago

The cloud which became the planet Earth began to shrink and to be very hot. As it heated up, it changed into a ball of liquid rock spinning in space.

4,000
million years
ago

Slowly, over millions of years, the ball of rock cooled down. A crust of solid rock hardened on the outside, but underneath the rock was still hot and liquid.

3,500
million years
ago

Thick clouds surrounded the Earth. When these cooled, rain began to fall. It rained for thousands of years and the rainwater made rivers and oceans.

How life began

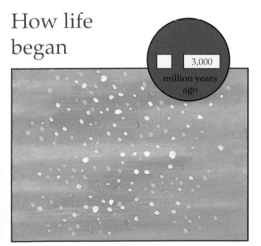

3,000
million years
ago

The first living things on planet Earth grew in the sea. They were neither animals nor plants. Scientists know very little about them because they were very tiny.

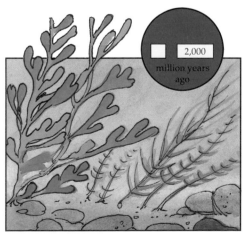

2,000
million years
ago

Very slowly, these tiny living things changed and became plants growing in the sea. There were no animals yet because there was no oxygen for them to breathe.

600
million years
ago

Plants make oxygen as they grow. When there was enough oxygen, animals began to form in the sea. Some of the first animals were jellyfish and sponges like these.

3

The fossil clues

People who study the plants and animals which lived millions of years ago are called paleontologists. They study fossils, which are all that remain of prehistoric life. A fossil is made when the remains of animals or plants slowly change to stone.

When scientists discover a plant or animal, they give it a Latin or Ancient Greek name so that people who speak different languages can use the same names. There is a list of what the names mean in English on the last page of this book.

How fossils are made

Fossils are made at the same time as the rock they are found in. Here is how it happens.

Rain and rivers wear away rocks and wash the sand and mud, called sediment, into the sea. This sediment slowly builds up to form thick layers on the sea floor.

When sea creatures die, their soft bodies rot away and their shells are buried in the sediment. After millions of years the layers of sediment are very deep and heavy.

Paleontologists travel all over the world looking for fossils. When they find them, they dig them out of the rock and take them back to the laboratory.

The sediment at the bottom is pressed down so hard that it becomes rock, called sedimentary rock. The shells leave a print of their shape in the rock.

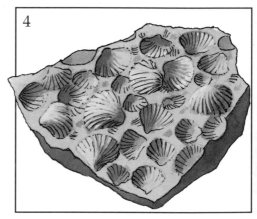

These prints made by shells are called fossils. Fossil prints of leaves and footprints are made like this too. Fossils of bones are made in a different way.

They study the fossil to find out what sort of plant or animal it was. Here they are measuring a giant ammonite which lived in the sea 150 million years ago.

Bones buried in the sand are slowly dissolved away. The space left is filled by tiny grains of sand which harden into a fossil, shaped like the animal's bones.

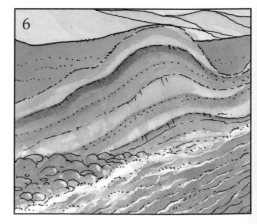

Movements in the Earth's crust lift the rocks above the sea. As the rocks wear away, the fossils of prehistoric plants and animals appear on their surface.

Plants and animals in the rock

Here are the fossil remains of some plants and animals. They have not been drawn to scale. In this book the name of each plant or animal is printed in *italics*. The name of the group the plant or animal belongs to is in ordinary type.

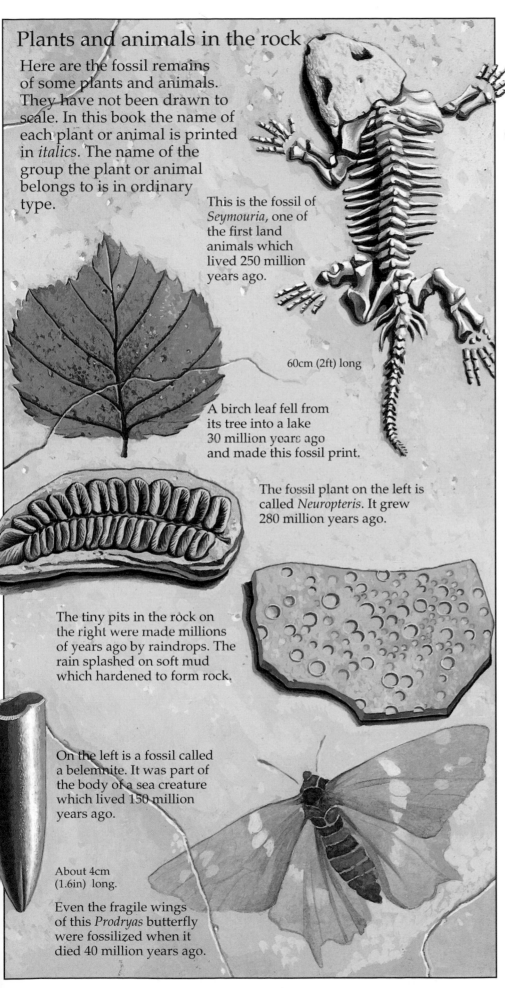

This is the fossil of *Seymouria*, one of the first land animals which lived 250 million years ago.

60cm (2ft) long

A birch leaf fell from its tree into a lake 30 million years ago and made this fossil print.

The fossil plant on the left is called *Neuropteris*. It grew 280 million years ago.

The tiny pits in the rock on the right were made millions of years ago by raindrops. The rain splashed on soft mud which hardened to form rock.

On the left is a fossil called a belemnite. It was part of the body of a sea creature which lived 150 million years ago.

About 4cm (1.6in) long.

Even the fragile wings of this *Prodryas* butterfly were fossilized when it died 40 million years ago.

Model fossils

You will need plaster of Paris, playdough, thin cardboard, soap or cooking oil, and some leaves.

Sticky tape

Make a flat piece of playdough big enough to take the leaf. Then make a ring of cardboard to fit around the leaf.

Press leaf flat.

Press the ring into the playdough and coat the leaf with soap or oil. Put the leaf inside the ring, pressing it gently so it lies flat.

Plaster about 2cm (0.8in) deep.

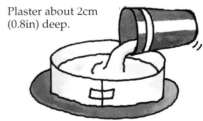

Mix a thin paste of plaster of Paris. Pour it over the leaf and let it set.

When the plaster is hard, take off the ring and peel away the playdough. Gently pull the leaf off the plaster. Try making model fossils of seashells too.

The first life

The land was dry and lifeless 550 million years ago. But the seas and lakes were full of plants and animals, like the ones here. Scientists studied fossils to find out what they looked like. Trilobites died out millions of years ago, but jellyfish, sponges and sea lilies still live in the sea.

Fossils of plants and animals which lived together at the same time are found in the same layer in the rock. Scientists can tell what the weather was like by looking at the type of plants that grew. Here is what they think life in the sea looked like, about 550 million years ago.

Reading rocks

Fossils are the same age as the sedimentary rock in which they are found. Scientists calculate how old the rocks are, and then know the age of the fossils too.

Sedimentary rock is made in layers. The layer of rock at the bottom formed first and so is the oldest. The fossils found there are older than those higher up.

Sponges are animals and they still live in the sea today. Their soft, fleshy bodies did not make good fossils.

Sea lilies are animals, not flowers. They catch food with their wavy arms.

This is an annelid worm. There are fossils of the trails and burrows these worms made in the sand.

Trilobites crawled on the sand, looking for food. Most were 2-10cm (1-4in) long, but some giant trilobites were 70cm (2ft 4in) long.

Fossils of trails made by trilobites have been found in the rocks.

These are called lamp shells because they look like a kind of ancient Roman lamp.

The name trilobite means "three-lobed" and describes the shape of the animal's body.

Fossil trilobites

Trilobites made good fossils because they had hard skin. Their antennae did not become fossils, because they were too soft, but marks on the fossil body show where they joined it. The trilobite's hard skin protected it from danger. Some trilobites could curl into a tight ball to protect themselves.

Jellyfish like these still live in the sea and catch food with their tentacles.

Fossil jellyfish

Jellyfish did not make good fossils because their bodies were too soft. This one left a print of its body shape in soft mud.

Make some trilobites

Cut out egg shape.

To make a model of a trilobite, first roll out a piece of playdough. Then cut out a flat, egg-shaped piece, which will become the trilobite's body.

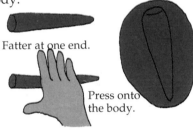

Fatter at one end.

Press onto the body.

Next, roll a carrot-shaped piece of playdough the same length as the egg shape. One end should be a bit fatter than the other. Press this along the middle of the body.

Press antennae onto body.

Scratch markings with pencil.

Roll a long, thin sausage shape and cut it in half to make two antennae. Then scratch markings on the trilobite with the point of a pencil.

Leaves stuck in playdough.

Carrot tops.

Sand

Pebbles

Make an underwater scene by putting the trilobites on some sand in a bowl. To make plants, cut the tops off carrots and put them in the water to sprout.

The first fish

For millions of years the seas stayed warm and calm. Trilobites still crawled over the sea floor, but there were new creatures too. Some had shells and others lived in a chalky skeleton of coral. All these animals are called invertebrates because they had no backbone.

As time passed, some animals developed backbones and became fish. Animals with backbones are called vertebrates. The way living things slowly change over long periods of time, is called evolution (see page 13).

Life in the sea

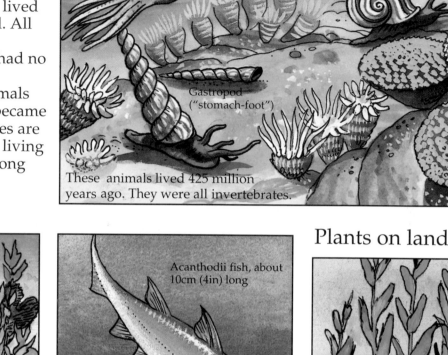

Cephalopod ("head-foot")

Coral

Gastropod ("stomach-foot")

These animals lived 425 million years ago. They were all invertebrates.

About 1m (3ft) long

The first animals with backbones were fish-like creatures called ostracoderms. They had thick, armoured skin and their name means "shell-skinned".

Acanthodii fish, about 10cm (4in) long

The first fish had no jaws, but later on fish had jaws with sharp teeth. They could swim very fast and chased other sea creatures to catch them for food.

Plants on land

Plants first grew on the land 400 million years ago on wet, marshy ground near water. Later, stronger plants grew and spread over the rest of the land.

The great drought

About 375 million years ago the weather became very hot. There were long seasons of drought and the lakes and rivers dried up in the hot sun.

Many fish died as the lakes shrank. Their bodies lay on the sun-baked mud and sand blew over them. It was so dry that their bodies did not rot away.

Fossil fish

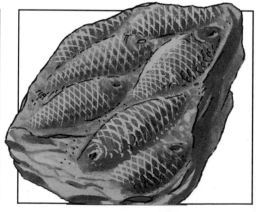

This is the fossil of a group of fish which died when the lakes dried up. Their bodies were so well preserved that you can even see the shape of the scales.

Prehistoric sea monster

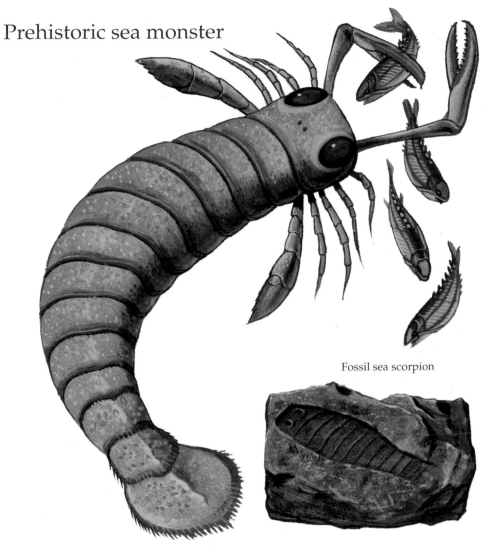

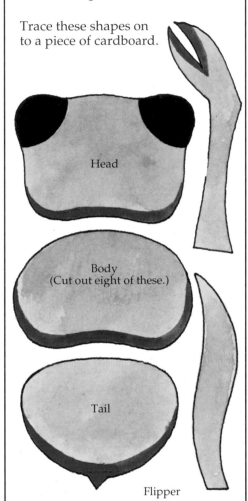

Make a sea scorpion

Here is how to make a wriggly cardboard model of a sea scorpion.

Trace these shapes on to a piece of cardboard.

Head

Body
(Cut out eight of these.)

Tail

Flipper

Fossil sea scorpion

This is a eurypterid, or sea scorpion, which lived 400 million years ago. It was about 3m (10ft) long and caught small creatures with its long pincers.

The sea scorpion was an invertebrate and so had no backbone. It had a hard skin which was jointed so that it could move. You can see the marks of its eyes.

Paint or crayon the shapes and then cut them out of the cardboard. Take one of the body pieces and staple or stitch it to the head as shown in the picture. Attach the other pieces and put the tail on the end. Staple the flippers to the side of the head and put the pincers on the front. To make the scorpion wriggle, twitch its tail.

Fish on land

This is *Eusthenopteron*. It had a lung as well as gills, so it could breathe on land. It also had strong bones in its fins with which it used to pull itself along the

ground. This meant the fish survived the drought because it was able to live on land and drag itself to a pool or stream. It was about 50cm (1ft 8in) long.

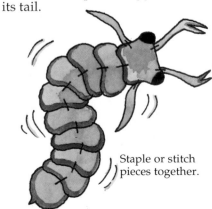

Staple or stitch pieces together.

Animals crawl onto land

The first creatures to live on land were fish, with lungs and strong fins. Through evolution, they slowly changed over the next few million years becoming more suited to living on the land. Their fins became legs, strong enough for walking, and their lungs grew bigger.

Animals which live on land but have to return to the water to lay their eggs are called amphibians. The first land animals on Earth were amphibians. The weather was hot and rainy then and there were plenty of pools where they could lay their eggs.

The first amphibian

One of the first amphibians on Earth was *Ichthyostega*. It measured about 1m (3ft) long and lived 360 million years ago. It had strong legs, and had feet with five toes, but its tail was like that of a fish. The *Ichthyostega's* legs were strong enough to carry it on land, but most of the time it probably stayed in the water, swimming and catching fish for food.

Did you know?

The coal we burn for heat and light is 300 million years old.

There have been cockroaches crawling around on Earth for 300 million years.

The largest flying insect that has ever existed was a giant *Meganeura*. It measured 70cm (2ft 4in) across the wings.

Coal often contains fossils of the leaves and plants that it is made of.

Insects

Meganeura

The first insects lived at this time too. This is the fossil of *Meganeura*, an insect which looked like a huge dragonfly. It lived near swamps and ate other insects.

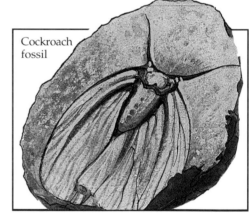

Cockroach fossil

This is the fossil of a cockroach which lived at the same time as the amphibians. Cockroaches and other insects were probably eaten by the amphibians.

The life of amphibians

The modern frog is an amphibian. Adults live on land and their lifecycle is the same as that of the first amphibians back in prehistory.

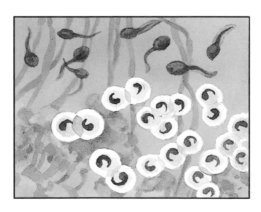

Frogs have to lay their eggs in water. The eggs have no shells and would dry up if they were laid on the land. The eggs hatch into tadpoles.

Tadpoles breathe through gills. Eventually their tails and gills disappear and legs and lungs appear. The adults can live on land.

Prehistoric forests

Thick forests covered the land about 300 million years ago. In these forests there were lakes and swamps full of rotting leaves and plants.

Giant clubmosses grew 30m (98ft) tall with trunks nearly 1m (3ft) across. Scars on the trunk were left by leaves which had dropped off.

Meganeura

This is the trunk of *Calamites*, a kind of horsetail which grew 18m (59ft) tall.

Amphibians lived near lakes and swamps in the forest, and ate fish or insects.

Cockroaches ate the leaves and rotting plants.

Horsetails like these still grow in marshy places today.

Mosses, ferns and liverworts grew on the wet ground.

How coal is made

Coal is made from plants which grew 300 million years ago. Dead branches and leaves fell into swamps and built up into a thick layer of rotting plants.

Later the swamps were covered by the sea. The rotting wood and leaves were buried under thick layers of mud and sand at the bottom of the sea.

The layers of sand and mud squashed the plants and changed them into coal. Now we dig into the ground for coal and burn it to make heat.

The first reptiles

About 280 million years ago the weather changed and became very hot and dry again. The swamps slowly dried up and most of the amphibians died.

Now a new kind of animal evolved. It had thick, scaly skin and laid eggs which were protected by a leathery shell. This type of animal is called a reptile. The lizards and snakes you see today are reptiles.

The new reptiles laid their eggs in the warm sand or in nests of rotting plants. The shell of the egg protected it from drying up in the hot sun.

Diadectes was one of the early reptiles. It measured about 2m (6ft 7in) from its nose to the end of its long tail. Fossils of its teeth show that it ate plants.

The legs stuck out on either side and did not support it very well. But they were strong enough to lift the body off the ground and take long steps.

Land animals of 240 million years ago

Gradually, over millions of years, some of the reptiles changed. They had different teeth, their legs were stronger and some of them had hair instead of scales. Animals which have hair and suckle their young are called mammals. Some reptiles' bodies had parts like those of mammals. They are called mammal-like reptiles.

Lystrosaurus was a mammal-like reptile, which lived in swamps and ate plants. It was about 1.5m (5ft) long.

Sauroctonus was a fierce mammal-like reptile. It had long, sharp teeth and ate other animals.

Euparkeria was a reptile which lived about 225 million years ago. It was about 1m (3ft) long and was the ancestor of some of the dinosaurs.

Thrinaxodon was a mammal-like reptile which had developed hair, but it probably still laid eggs. It was about the size of a cat.

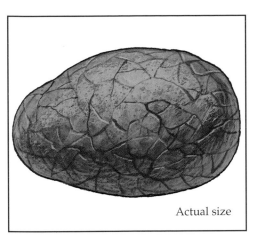

Actual size

This fossil egg is about 225 million years old. The shell dried and cracked before it became a fossil. Scientists do not know which reptile laid it.

Edaphosaurus was a reptile which lived 250 million years ago. It was about 3m (10ft) long. The sail on its back was made of long bones covered with skin.

It may have used the sail to keep its body at the right temperature. When it was cold it heated up quickly by turning the sail to the heat of the sun.

What is a reptile?

Reptiles are animals which have scaly skin and lay eggs with shells. They are cold-blooded, which means they cannot control the temperature of their body.

What is evolution?

The idea that animals and plants slowly change over millions of years to become different types, is called evolution. It was first thought of by the scientist Charles Darwin, over 100 years ago. Some people disagreed with his ideas.

Darwin showed that no two animals of the same type are identical. (For example, one fox will not be exactly the same as another fox.) Some are taller, or stronger, or differ in other ways. This will affect how well they survive.

Those that are better able to survive have more chance of becoming adults, and so will have more babies than other animals. These babies will be like their parents and better able to survive too. Slowly, the animals less able to survive, die out. This process is called "the survival of the fittest". It explains how animals evolve and become better suited to their surroundings.

About 375 million years ago the weather changed and there were long, dry seasons. One kind of fish, called *Eusthenopteron*, (see also

Over the next few million years, some of the descendants of *Eusthenopteron* evolved even stronger fins.

page 9) was able to survive because it had strong fins and could drag itself across the land to find pools. Many of the other fish died.

Eventually, about 360 million years ago, some animals evolved legs. These were the first amphibians.

The age of dinosaurs

Dinosaurs were a group of reptiles which lived from 230 million years to 65 million years ago. Paleontologists have found thousands of fossils which show what dinosaurs looked like and how they lived. There are dinosaur fossils of bones and teeth, footprints and skin, and even fossil eggs with baby dinosaurs inside.

The name dinosaur means "terrible lizard". There were dinosaurs on the Earth for about 165 million years, which is 70 times longer than people have lived on Earth.

The first dinosaurs

Herrerasaurus is the earliest known dinosaur and was found in 230 million year old rocks in Argentina. It was about 3m (10ft) long, had sharp teeth and ate meat.

Coelophysis was another early dinosaur. It measured about 2m (6ft 7in) long. It walked on its back legs and had a long tail to help it balance. It had sharp teeth and ate meat.

Prehistoric footprints

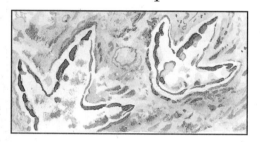

Fossil footprints of *Megalosaurus*, a huge meat-eating dinosaur, show the shape of its three toes. The footprints were made when it walked on soft mud. The mud was baked by the sun and later covered by sand. This hardened to form rock which still had the shape of the footprints in it.

Fossil skin

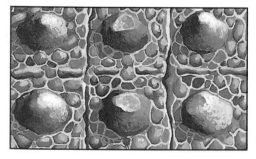

This is a piece of fossil skin from the *Euoplocephalus*. This dinosaur had thick, scaly skin with spikes to protect it.

You can see the shape of the scales and bony spikes. The fossil is the colour of stone and not the real skin colour.

Baby dinosaurs

Most baby dinosaurs hatched from eggs. Some kinds laid their eggs on bare ground. Other kinds laid them in hollows scooped out of the sand and then covered the eggs with sand. Scientists have also discovered nests in the ground with raised rims made of mud. *Maiasaura* mother dinosaurs built nests that were 2m (6ft 6in) wide, and fed their young with plants until they were strong enough to leave the nest and look for their own food.

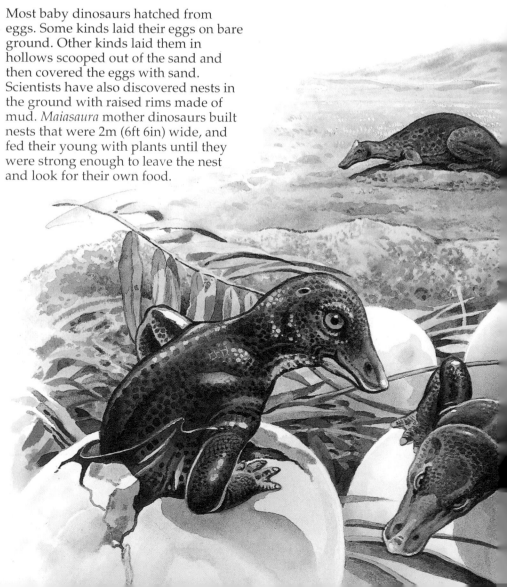

Dinosaur ancestors

Millerosaurus
30cm (1ft) long

Shansisuchus
2m (6ft 7in) long

Saltoposuchus
120cm (4ft) long

The ancestors of the dinosaurs were reptiles like *Millerosaurus* which lived 250 million years ago. They crawled with their legs stuck out from the sides.

Shansisuchus was a reptile which lived 225 million years ago. Its legs were tucked under its body. They lifted it well off the ground, although it was heavy.

Saltoposuchus was the ancestor of some of the two-legged dinosaurs. Dinosaurs had stronger legs than the early reptiles and had long tails to help them balance.

Monster quiz

The letters in these reptiles' names have been mixed up. Can you decide what the names ought to be? The answers are on the last page of this book.

1 Donoguani - This one had spikes on its thumbs.

2 Pertosaurs - These were flying reptiles.

3 Gosetsaurus - This dinosaur had spikes on its tail.

4 Rantynosaurus - A very fierce dinosaur.

5 Chabriosaurus - The biggest and heaviest dinosaur.

6 Harodsaurs - These dinosaurs had bony crests on their heads.

Finding dinosaur fossils

Paleontologists hunt for fossil remains in sedimentary rocks (see page 4) as this is the only type of rock where fossils form.

You can find fossils too. A good place to look is at the bottom of cliffs (see page 24).

Finding a dinosaur fossil is always exciting and sometimes it may be a new dinosaur that no one has discovered before. Fossils can be bones, or simply a trace such as the imprint of a dinosaur foot in mud. It can take many years to put a skeleton together from all the bones.

Paleontologists label each bone and then photograph and draw the fossil in the rock. This helps them when they try to put the bones together.

The fossil bones are very fragile. They have to be wrapped in wet tissue and then covered with strips of cloth dipped in plaster of Paris to protect them.

Making mistakes

Sometimes scientists make mistakes when they reconstruct fossil dinosaur skeletons. At first they thought *Iguanodon* had a horn on its nose.

Later they realized that *Iguanodon* had no horn but a spike on each of its thumbs. Scientists are more experienced now and make fewer mistakes.

Fossil skeleton

The picture below shows the fossil skeleton of the dinosaur *Plateosaurus*. The picture on the right is a reconstruction of the dinosaur.

Of course it may not have looked exactly like this. It is only what paleontologists think *Plateosaurus* looked like when it was alive.

In museums, you can sometimes see wires holding the skeleton in a life-like pose. If it is a very rare fossil, fibreglass models of the bones are shown instead of the real fossil bones.

When paleontologists have cleaned all the fossil bones, they fit them together to make the skeleton. Broken bones have to be mended and the pieces stuck together like a jig-saw puzzle. If any of the bones are missing, then bones from another dinosaur of the same type have to be used.

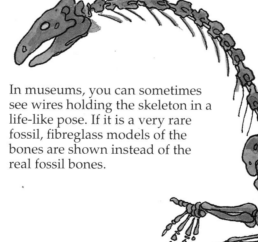

3

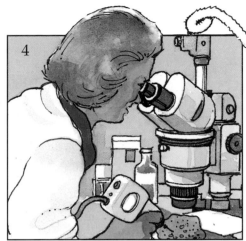

4

Sometimes large fossils are almost completely buried in solid rock. This means the whole block of rock has to be cut out and taken back to the laboratory.

The rock around the fossils can be removed with tiny needle-like drills, or washed away with chemicals. Great care is taken not to damage the fossil.

The living dinosaur

Plateosaurus ("flat lizard") was about 6m (20ft) long. It was one of the first plant eating dinosaurs and lived about 220 million years ago.

Clues on the fossil bones help paleontologists reconstruct what a living dinosaur looked like. All animal bones have lumps and scars which show where the muscles joined them. By studying the lumps on the fossil bones, scientists can find out the shape of the dinosaur's muscles.

Fossils of dinosaur skin show that it was thick and scaly skin, like a modern crocodile's. No fossils show us what colour the skin was. Many large, modern reptiles, such as the crocodile, are greenish brown, so perhaps dinosaurs were greenish brown too.

Pipecleanosaurus

We have called our model dinosaur Pipecleanosaurus because it is made of pipe-cleaners.

Twist ends together.

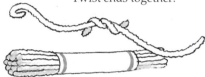

Join two pipe-cleaners by twisting the ends. Then bend them to make the curve of the dinosaur's spine.

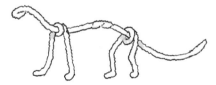

Bend two more pipe-cleaners in half for the legs. Twist them around the spine. Then bend them at the knees and ankles.

To make ribs, cut one piece of pipe-cleaner 8cm (3.5in) long, two 7cm (3in), two 6cm (2.5in)and two 5cm (2in) long. Then twist them around the spine.

Now bend the ribs to curve them in slightly. You could make models of other dinosaur skeletons in this book.

What dinosaurs ate

Some dinosaurs ate plants and others ate meat. The giant dinosaurs, such as *Brachiosaurus*, ate only plants and must have eaten nearly a tonne (ton) of leaves every day to stay alive. Animals which eat plants are called herbivores and animals that eat meat are called carnivores.

Carnivorous dinosaurs had long, sharp claws for attacking their prey and pointed teeth for tearing the meat. The herbivores had to defend themselves from the fierce carnivorous dinosaurs which attacked them for food.

Plant-eating dinosaurs

Camarasaurus

Iguanodon was about 5m (16ft) tall.

Pinacosaurus

The herbivores were not all competing for the same food. The giant dinosaurs could reach the leaves in the treetops and the small dinosaurs ate the plants at ground level.

about 5.5m (18ft) long.

Fighting off the carnivores

Some herbivores lived together in packs to defend themselves from carnivores. Here are some of the other ways they defended themselves.

This herbivore is called *Euoplocephalus*. It stunned its attackers with the bony club on its tail. It measured 5m (16ft) from nose to tail.

Polacanthus had thick scaly skin with spikes on its back and bony plates on its tail. Its name means "many spined".

Deinonychus was a carnivore. It had huge claws with which it held and killed its prey.

Deinonychus was 2m (6ft 7in) long and the name means "terrible claw".

Stegosaurus had large, bony plates growing from the skin on its back, and spikes like daggers on its tail. Its plates were like roof tiles and its name means "roof-lizard".

About 10m (33ft) long.

A fierce carnivore

Tyrannosaurus rex was the largest carnivore. Its name means "king of the tyrant reptiles". This huge dinosaur weighed over 8 tonnes (7.9 tons) and was nearly 15m (49ft) long. Most carnivores moved on their hind legs and could run fast to catch their prey.

Tyrannosaurus rex had very short front arms. Here, it is attacking a sauropod dinosaur called *Alamosaurus.*

How we know

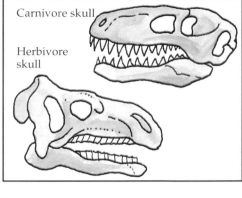

Carnivore skull

Herbivore skull

We can tell what dinosaurs ate by looking at their teeth. Carnivores had long, sharp teeth, but the herbivores' teeth were flat for chewing tough plants.

Dinosaur dropping

Fossils of dinosaur droppings are called coprolites. Scientists can tell what the dinosaurs ate by grinding the coprolites and examining the dust.

Hypsilophodon was a small dinosaur about 60cm (2ft) long. It had long legs and could run fast to escape.

The giant dinosaurs

The giant dinosaurs are the largest land animals that have ever lived and belonged to a group called sauropods. They had four legs, a small head and a huge bulky body. Their necks and tails were very long.

Heavy dinosaurs

The *Brachiosaurus* (there are two pictured here) was one of the biggest dinosaurs. It was about 25m (82ft) long and weighed 29-54 tonnes (29-53 tons). The largest dinosaur discovered so far is *Seismosaurus* which was 39-50m (128-164ft) long. Its name means "earth-shaking lizard".

Why were they so big?

Dinosaurs were probably cold-blooded. This means that their body temperature was controlled by the heat of the sun. If the weather was cool, the dinosaurs got cold. But some of the dinosaurs were so big that it took them a very long time to cool. Their great size kept them warm and this was probably one of the reasons they were so big.

In herds for safety

Apatosaurus used to be called Brontosaurus. These dinosaurs stayed together in herds to protect themselves from attack by the meat-eating dinosaurs. *Apatosaurus* means "deceptive lizard". It was about 21m (69ft) long, nearly as long as a railway carriage, and weighed about 20 tonnes (19.7 tons). Compared to the size of its body, it had a smaller brain than any other animal.

Apatosaurus

How they moved

Sauropods walked on all fours, but could rear up on their back legs to feed or fight. They had legs like pillars. The *Diplodocus* pictured here had strong front legs and shoulders with powerful muscles. The pelvis was strong too, to support the long back legs. The bones in their legs were very strong, but their spines were hollow

to make them lighter. A sauropod hand was similar to an elephant's front foot, but it had one sharp claw and some smaller nails.

Shoulder

Pelvis

Pillar-like legs

Measure some dinosaurs

To see how big some of the dinosaurs were, pace out their lengths in a park or playground. Your pace is probably about 1m (3ft) long. (If you want to be exact you can measure it.) To measure *Diplodocus*, which was 27m (89ft) long, mark where you start and take 27 paces. Then look back and see just how huge it really was.

Smallest dinosaur

Compsognathus was the smallest dinosaur. It was about the size of a crow. It fed on insects and small reptiles and could run very fast.

Diplodocus

Diplodocus measured 27m (89ft) from its nose to the tip of its very long, whip-like tail and weighed only 10-11 tonnes (10-11 tons). *Diplodocus* was a plant eater.

The dinosaur's brain was no bigger than a hen's egg and it had another nerve control between its legs. This worked the back legs and tail.

Horned and crested dinosaurs

Some dinosaurs had strange crests of bone on their heads. They belonged to a group called the hadrosaurs. The crest probably worked as a very sensitive nose which helped the hadrosaurs smell enemies from far away.

Another group of dinosaurs had horns on their heads and bony shields around their necks. These were the ceratopsians.

Hadrosaurs and ceratopsians were plant-eating dinosaurs. They probably developed their special heads as protection against the carnivores.

Duck-billed dinosaurs

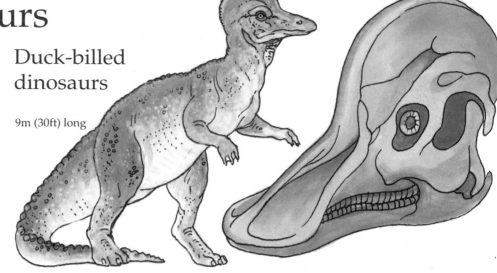

9m (30ft) long

Corythosaurus was a hadrosaur with a crest shaped like a helmet. The crest was made of bone with air tubes inside leading to the animal's lungs.

The hadrosaurs are also called duck-billed dinosaurs, because their jaws ended in a horny, toothless beak. They used this to clip leaves from the trees.

Horned dinosaurs

11m (36ft) long

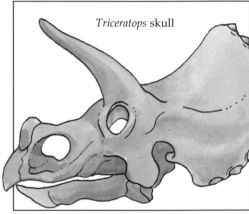

Triceratops skull

Triceratops was one of the ceratopsian dinosaurs. It had three horns, one on its nose and one over each eye. Around its neck it had a long shield of bone.

At the end of its mouth it had a beak to cut through the stems of plants. It ate very tough leaves and had special sharp, scissor-like teeth to chop them.

This is the skull of *Triceratops*. Ceratopsians had strong jaw muscles to help them chew tough plants. The bony neck shield supported the jaw muscles.

Bone-heads

9m (30ft) long

The bone-headed dinosaurs had thick skulls with bone about 20cm (8in) thick on top. This probably protected them during a fight.

These dinosaurs lived together in herds. The males may have fought each other to prove which of them was the strongest.

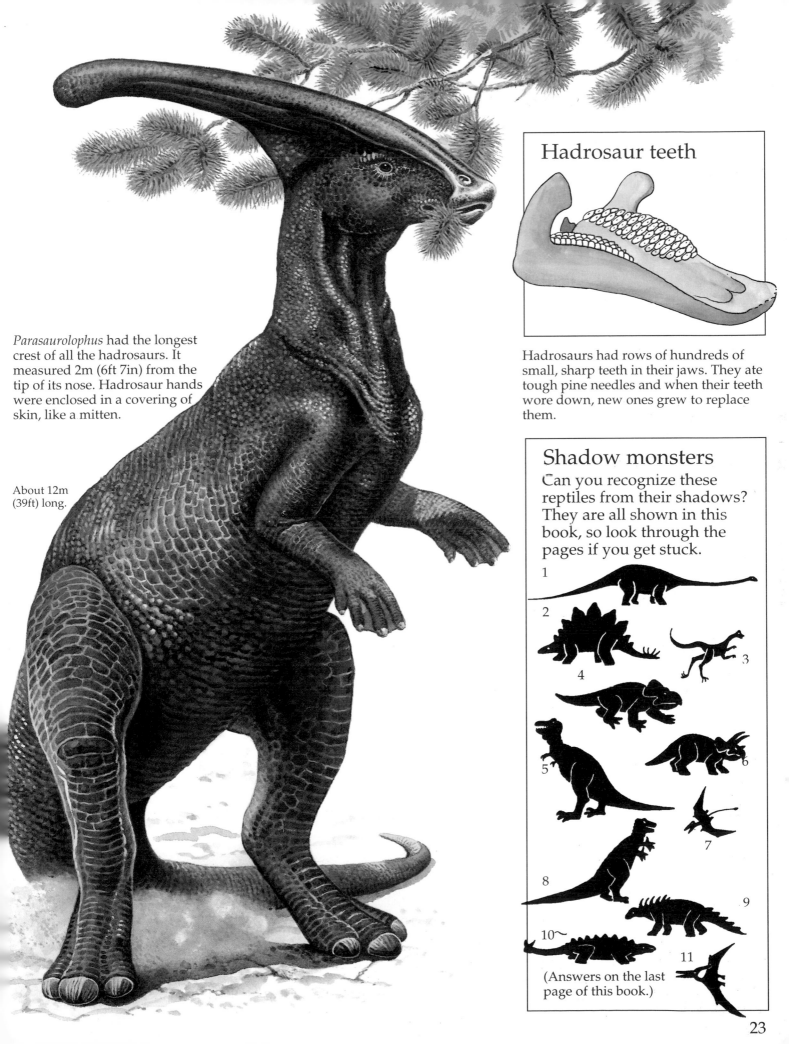

Parasaurolophus had the longest crest of all the hadrosaurs. It measured 2m (6ft 7in) from the tip of its nose. Hadrosaur hands were enclosed in a covering of skin, like a mitten.

About 12m (39ft) long.

Hadrosaur teeth

Hadrosaurs had rows of hundreds of small, sharp teeth in their jaws. They ate tough pine needles and when their teeth wore down, new ones grew to replace them.

Shadow monsters

Can you recognize these reptiles from their shadows? They are all shown in this book, so look through the pages if you get stuck.

1
2
3
4
5
6
7
8
9
10
11

(Answers on the last page of this book.)

Sea monsters

At the same time as the dinosaurs, there were huge creatures living in the sea. These creatures evolved from reptiles which lived on the land 280 million years ago. Over millions of years their bodies became smooth and streamlined to suit life in the sea, and their legs became flippers.

These sea creatures were reptiles, but they did not lay eggs. There are fossils of sea reptiles with babies inside them, which shows that they gave birth to live young. To the right you can see three different kinds of sea reptile.

A famous fossil find

Mary Anning lived in Dorset, England about 150 years ago, in a small village by the sea. Mary used to go fossil hunting along the beach with her father.

They found lots of fossils of ammonites and when she was eleven she found a nearly perfect fossil of an ichthyosaur.

Mary Anning was the first person to discover a complete plesiosaur fossil. Her fossils are now in the Natural History Museum, London.

Ichthyosaurs were very fast swimmers. They had strong tail fins and could probably leap out of the water. Their long jaws were full of sharp teeth and they ate fish and shellfish. There were many different kinds of ichthyosaur, which means "fish lizard". Some of them were about 12m (39ft) long.

Pliosaurs had short necks and large heads with lots of sharp teeth. They had strong flippers and could dive deep into the water to catch fish and ammonites.

Fossil ichthyosaur

This fossil of an ichthyosaur is so well preserved that you can see the outline of its skin. It had very large eyes so that it could see in the dark water.

It used its tail fin for swimming and steered with the fins on its sides. The fin on its back stopped its body from rolling from side to side as it swam.

Fossil teeth marks

This is the fossil shell of an ammonite, a sea creature which lived at the same time as the sea reptiles. This one has marks of a sea reptile's teeth on it.

Plesiosaurs had very long necks. They pulled themselves through the water with large, flat flippers and could swing their heads from side to side when looking for fish. Some were about 12m (39ft) long.

Plesiosaur skeleton

This is a model of the fossil skeleton of a plesiosaur. These sea reptiles had small skulls and some of them had as many as 76 bones in their long necks.

The plesiosaurs and other sea reptiles evolved from land animals. Their leg bones changed shape and became paddles for swimming in the water.

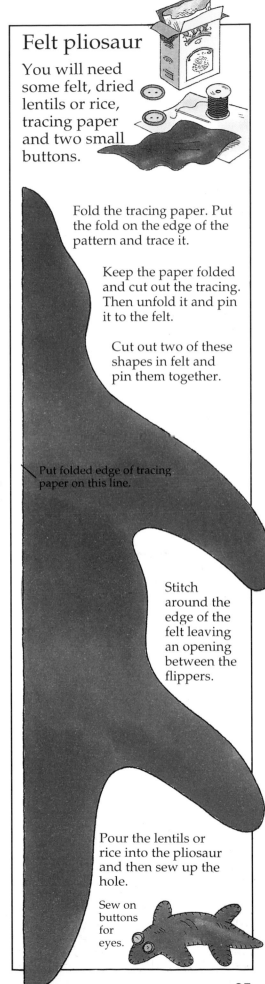

Felt pliosaur

You will need some felt, dried lentils or rice, tracing paper and two small buttons.

Fold the tracing paper. Put the fold on the edge of the pattern and trace it.

Keep the paper folded and cut out the tracing. Then unfold it and pin it to the felt.

Cut out two of these shapes in felt and pin them together.

Put folded edge of tracing paper on this line.

Stitch around the edge of the felt leaving an opening between the flippers.

Pour the lentils or rice into the pliosaur and then sew up the hole.

Sew on buttons for eyes.

Flying reptiles

The flying reptiles are called pterosaurs. They lived at the same time as the dinosaurs. Some scientists think they were not reptiles, but were warm-blooded and furry.

The pterosaurs were not very strong fliers. Their wings were made of leathery skin supported by the fourth finger which had grown very long. They probably glided with outstretched wings and swooped down to catch fish or insects. If they were in danger, they could escape into the air, out of reach of the dinosaurs.

Dimorphodon lived about 190 million years ago and was one of the first pterosaurs. It measured nearly 2m (6ft 7in) across its wings and had a long tail.

Like the other pterosaurs it had claws on its wings and large back claws. Its head was large and clumsy and it had sharp teeth in its beak-like jaws.

Toothless gliders

Pteranodon was one of the largest flying reptiles. It measured 8m (26ft) across its wings, but only weighed about 20kg (44lb). Its claws were not very strong and it probably had difficulty moving on land.

It had a long, bony crest on the back of its head and a pointed beak with no teeth. It may have soared over the sea, looking for fish which it caught in its beak-like jaws and fed to its young.

Fossil pterosaur

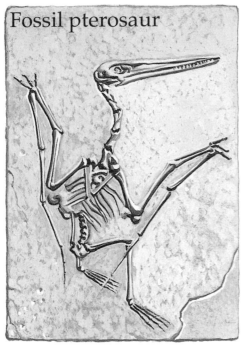

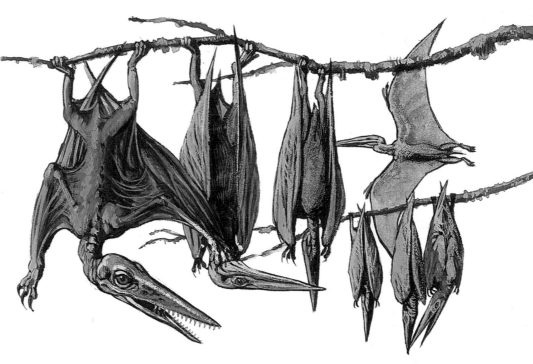

This is the fossil skeleton of *Pterodactylus*, one of the smallest pterosaurs. It shows the bones of the long fourth finger which supported the wing. You can see the teeth in its beak too. Its head was flat on top with not much space for the brain.

Pterodactylus was about the size of a starling. They lived together in flocks and probably slept hanging upside-down in trees or caves. They lived near the sea and ate insects, which they probably snapped up in their jaws as they flew.

New discoveries

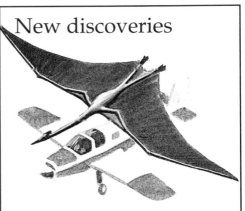

A fossil of the largest flying creature that has ever existed was found in 1975, in Texas, USA. It was a pterosaur with a wing-span of about 12m (39ft), which is larger than a two-seater aeroplane. This pterosaur has been named *Quetzalcoatlus*. It probably lived inland and fed on dead animals, like vultures.

Hairy pterosaur

Sometimes paleontologists find fossils which change all their ideas about an animal. In Kazakhstan, in what used to be the USSR, they found the fossil of a pterosaur, in 1966. It looks as though it was covered with fluffy hair.

Some scientists disagree about the hair. They think it may have been something like hair, which kept the pterosaurs warm or helped them to fly.

Rhamphorhynchus measured about 2m (6ft 7in) across the wings and had a long neck and head. Its tail ended in a diamond-shaped flap of skin which acted as a rudder and helped it to steer.

The bones of *Rhamphorhynchus* and other pterosaurs were hollow and filled with air. This made them light so they could glide more easily. Pterosaurs laid eggs but no nests have been found.

The first bird

All the birds which are on Earth today are descended from the dinosaurs. The first bird is called *Archaeopteryx* and it lived 150 million years ago. *Archaeopteryx* developed from small dinosaurs like *Compsognathus*. Its skeleton was like a reptile's, but fossils show that it had feathers, so it was a true bird.

Archaeopteryx was about the size of a crow. It lived in woodlands and ate berries and insects. Paleontologists think it could not fly very well. It probably climbed trees and then glided to the ground.

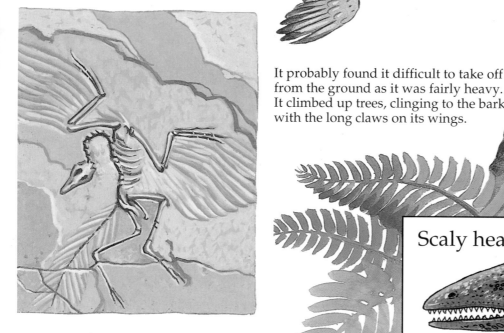

Archaeopteryx had strong claws. These helped it to grip branches and perch in trees. Its long tail kept it steady as it flew or glided down from the trees.

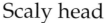

It probably found it difficult to take off from the ground as it was fairly heavy. It climbed up trees, clinging to the bark with the long claws on its wings.

Feathered fossil

This fossil of *Archaeopteryx* shows the feathers on the wings and tail very clearly. It had teeth in its jaw like a reptile, and a long bony tail. Like modern birds, it had hollow bones to make it lighter. The name *Archaeopteryx* means "ancient wing".

Scaly head

Archaeopteryx's head was covered with scaly skin like the dinosaurs'. On the rest of its body the scales had become feathers.

The end of the dinosaurs

About 65 million years ago, the dinosaurs became extinct. All the pterosaurs and the sea reptiles died out too.

No one knows exactly why, but scientists think perhaps they could not adapt to changes taking place in the climate.

When dinosaurs were alive the weather was warm all year long. About 65 million years ago, it became cooler with cold winters. Dinosaurs may have died out when the Earth got cooler, as they were cold-blooded and needed the sunshine to keep them warm.

Some scientists think that the dinosaurs became extinct because the Earth, gradually became cooler due to great movements in the rocks. Other scientists think dust clouds blocking out the sun's light may have caused the Earth to cool down. These clouds could have come from volcanic eruptions or a meteorite crashing onto the Earth's surface.

The survivors

Tuatara lizards lived at the same time as the dinosaurs. There are very few tuataras living now and they may soon become extinct themselves.

This is a mammal called *Protictis* which lived about 60 million years ago. Mammals are warm-blooded and they survived when the dinosaurs died out.

Great Tit

Mistle Thrush

Bullfinch

The birds that live today are the true descendants of dinosaurs. They evolved from the first bird, *Archaeopteryx*, which developed from a small kind of dinosaur.

Living reptiles

Many different kinds of reptiles live today. Many of them are threatened with extinction because people kill them for their beautiful skins or shells.

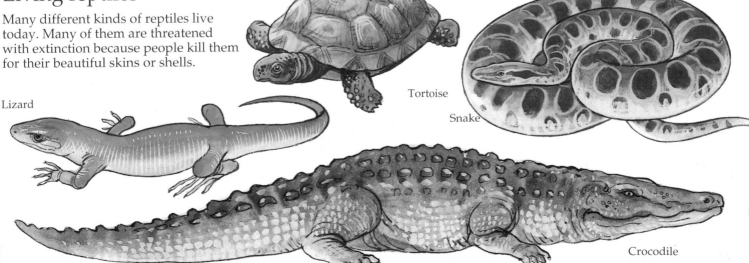

Lizard

Tortoise

Snake

Crocodile

Time chart

65 million years ago

CRETACEOUS

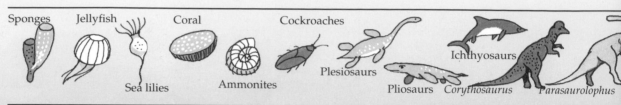

Sponges Jellyfish Coral Cockroaches

Sea lilies Ammonites Plesiosaurs Ichthyosaurs

Pliosaurs *Corythosaurus* *Parasaurolophus*

145 million years ago

JURASSIC

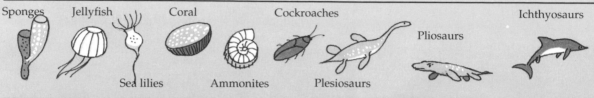

Sponges Jellyfish Coral Cockroaches Ichthyosaurs

Pliosaurs

Sea lilies Ammonites Plesiosaurs

203 million years ago

TRIASSIC

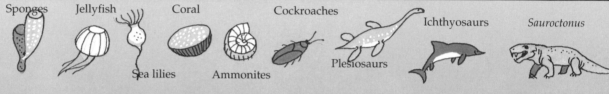

Sponges Jellyfish Coral Cockroaches Ichthyosaurs *Sauroctonus*

Plesiosaurs

Sea lilies Ammonites

245 million years ago

PERMIAN

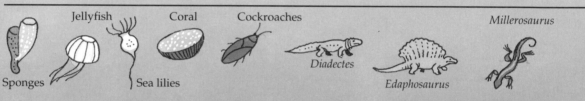

Jellyfish Coral Cockroaches *Millerosaurus*

Diadectes

Sponges Sea lilies *Edaphosaurus*

290 million years ago

CARBONIFEROUS

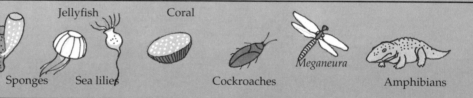

Trilobites Jellyfish Coral

Meganeura

Sponges Sea lilies Cockroaches Amphibians

362 million years ago

DEVONIAN

Trilobites Jellyfish Coral Ostracoderms

Ichthyostega

Sponges Sea lilies Sea scorpions *Eusthenopteron*

408 million years ago

SILURIAN

Trilobites Jellyfish First land plants Ostracoderms

Sea lilies Coral

Sponges Sea scorpions First fish

440 million years ago

ORDOVICIAN

Trilobites Jellyfish

Coral

Ostracoderms

Sponges Sea lilies

500 million years ago

CAMBRIAN

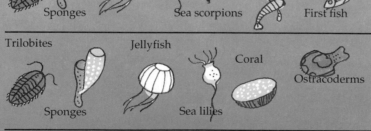

Trilobites Jellyfish Coral

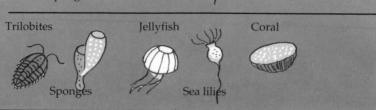

Sponges Sea lilies

570 million years ago

How this chart works

This time chart shows some of the animals which lived between 570 and 65 million years ago. It starts with the oldest animals at the bottom and works up to the more recent animals.

Paleontologists' time charts start at the bottom because this is how they find the fossils. The oldest fossils are in the deepest layers of rock with the newer fossils in the layers above.

At the side of the chart are the dates when the animals lived and the names of the different periods of prehistory.

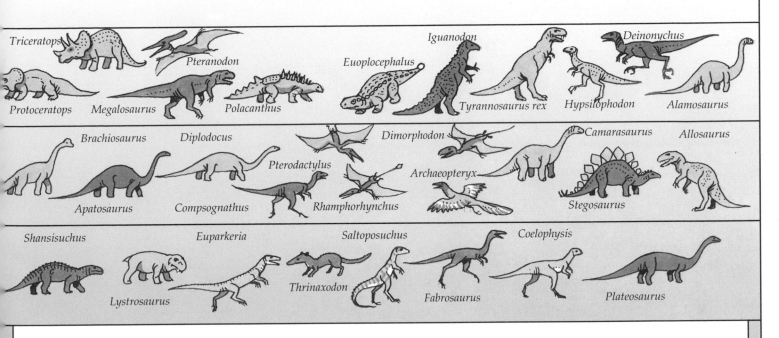

Triceratops
Pteranodon
Protoceratops
Megalosaurus
Polacanthus
Euoplocephalus
Iguanodon
Tyrannosaurus rex
Deinonychus
Hypsilophodon
Alamosaurus

Brachiosaurus
Diplodocus
Dimorphodon
Camarasaurus
Allosaurus
Apatosaurus
Compsognathus
Pterodactylus
Rhamphorhynchus
Archaeopteryx
Stegosaurus

Shansisuchus
Euparkeria
Saltoposuchus
Coelophysis
Lystrosaurus
Thrinaxodon
Fabrosaurus
Plateosaurus

Prehistory words

Ammonites
Sea creatures with coiled shells which lived 150 million years ago.

Amphibians
Animals, such as frogs, which live on land and lay their eggs in water.

Carnivores
Animals which eat meat.

Ceratopsians
Dinosaurs with horns and shields of bone around their necks.

Coprolite
Fossil animal dropping.

Dinosaurs
A group of reptiles which lived from 230 million to 65 million years ago.

Evolution
The way animals slowly change over a very long time to become different kinds of animals.

Fossils
Remains of ancient plants and animals preserved in the rocks.

Hadrosaurs
A group of dinosaurs, most of which had crests on their heads.

Herbivores
Animals which eat plants.

Ichthyosaurs
Swimming reptiles with fish-shaped bodies.

Invertebrates
Animals which do not have backbones.

Mammals
Animals which have fur, give birth to babies and can control their own body temperature.

Mammal-like reptiles
Reptiles which have some parts of their body like a mammal.

Ostracoderms
Fish-like sea creatures with thick, armoured skin which lived 400 million years ago.

Paleontologist
A scientist who studies fossils to find out about prehistoric plants and animals.

Paleontology
The study of prehistoric plants and animals.

Plesiosaurs
Reptiles with long necks which swam with four paddle-like legs.

Pliosaurs
Reptiles with short necks which swam with four paddle-like legs.

Pterosaurs
Flying reptiles with wings made of skin.

Reptiles
Animals which have scaly skin, lay eggs and cannot control their body temperature.

Sauropods
Very large, four-legged, herbivorous dinosaurs.

Sedimentary rock
Made from sand and mud which have been pressed down very hard and changed to rock.

Trilobites
Sea creatures with hard skin which lived 550 million years ago.

Vertebrates
Animals which have backbones.

Going further

Finding fossils

If you find a fossil, try and identify it by using a book, such as Fossils, Minerals and Rocks: collection and preservation, by R. Croucher and A.R. Woolley (British Museum/Cambridge University Press). If you cannot identify your fossil from a book, you could take it to your local museum or send it to the Natural History Museum, Cromwell Road, London, SW7 5BD. Pack the fossil carefully to make sure that it does not break and tell the museum where you found it.

Books

Digging up Dinosaurs. Aliki (The Bodley Head)
The Prehistoric Age. The British Museum (Quadriga NST International)
A Spotters Guide to Dinosaurs. D.B. Norman (Usborne Publishing)
Dinosaurs and How They Lived. S. Parker (Dorling Kindersley)
Where Did Dinosaurs Go? (Usborne Publishing)

Natural History Museum (London)

There is a large collection of fossil dinosaurs in the Natural History Museum in London.

Index

In this index, the English meanings of the Latin and Greek scientific names are in brackets. The names of individual plants and animals are written in italics and the names of groups of animals are in ordinary type.

Quiz answers

The reptiles in the monster quiz on page 15 are: 1. Iguanodon; 2. Pterosaurs; 3. Stegosaurus; 4. Tyrannosaurus; 5. Brachiosaurus; 6. Hadrosaurs.

The shadow monsters on page 23 are: 1. Diplodocus; 2. Stegosaurus; 3. Compsognathus; 4. Protoceratops; 5. Tyrannosaurus rex; 6. Triceratops; 7. Rhamphorhynchus; 8. Iguanodon; 9. Polacanthus; 10. Scolosaurus; 11. Pteranodon.

This edition published in 1993 by Usborne Publishing Ltd, Usborne House, 83-85 Saffron Hill, London EC1N 8RT, England. Based on a previous edition first published in 1977. Copyright © 1993, 1985, 1977 Usborne Publishing Ltd.

UE

Printed in Portugal.